# It's Candy Time!

based on the teleplay by
Evan Gore and Heather Lombard
adapted by Adam Beechen
illustrated by Tom LaPadula
and Barry Goldberg

Ready-to-Read

Simon Spotlight/Nickelodeon
New York    London    Toronto    Sydney

Based on the TV series *The Adventures of Jimmy Neutron, Boy Genius*®
as seen on Nickelodeon®

SIMON SPOTLIGHT
An imprint of Simon & Schuster Children's Publishing Division
1230 Avenue of the Americas
New York, NY 10020

Manufactured in the United States of America

First Edition
2 4 6 8 10 9 7 5 3 1

Library of Congress Cataloging-in-Publication Data
Beechen, Adam.
It's Candy Time! / by Adam Beechen.–1st ed.
p. cm.–(Ready-to-read. Level 2; #6)
Based on the TV series The adventures of Jimmy Neutron, boy genius. As seen on Nickelodeon®
Summary: When the residents of Retroville become addicted to the candy that Jimmy invents,
he attempts to solve the problem.
ISBN 0-689-85849-3
[1. Candy–Fiction. 2. Inventors–Fiction.]
I. Adventures of Jimmy Neutron, boy genius (Television program) II. Title. III. Series.
PZ7.B383It 2004
[E]–dc21
2002014992

Carl and Sheen could not decide which treat to buy at the Candy Bar.

"I want something gummy . . . no, crunchy," Sheen said.

"I want something sweet . . . no, salty," Carl said.

"I wish there was one candy
that had all the best flavors,"
Sheen said, sighing.
Jimmy smiled. "A mega-candy, huh?
I can invent that!"

Back in his lab, Jimmy filled test tubes with every flavor in the world.

"Get ready for an adventure in taste!"
Jimmy shouted, pushing buttons.
His candy-making machine rattled
and rumbled! When it was done,
Jimmy opened the door to reveal
one small piece of candy.

"Here, guys," Jimmy said, splitting
  the piece of candy in half.
"I never eat my own inventions."
  Carl and Sheen grabbed the candy
  and gave it a try.
"Yuck," his friends cried,
  spitting out the candy.
"I guess I should keep trying,"
  Jimmy said.

The next day Jimmy brought a bag
of new candy to school.
"I worked all night and tried
thousands of recipes," Jimmy said
to Carl and Sheen.

Miss Fowl saw Jimmy talking and
asked him to share his candy with
the whole class.
Everyone thought the candy was
the best thing they had ever eaten.
"These are as cool as me,"
Nick said.
Even Cindy liked the candy.
"They are okay," she admitted,
"if you like your candy sugary,
tangy, crunchy . . . and delicious!"

That night Jimmy went to bed
happy that he had made the
perfect candy.
He woke up in the middle of the
night to find Carl and Sheen
standing over his bed!
"Hi, Jimmy," they said, drooling.
"Do you have any more candy?"

"No, but I can make some,"
Jimmy told them.
"It will take about three hours."
"Three hours?!" voices yelled
in through his window.
Jimmy ran over and looked outside.
Everyone from his class was waiting
on his lawn!

"I will never bully you again,"
Butch promised.
"I will wear a 'Neutron is a Genius'
T-shirt," Cindy yelled.
"Leaping leptons," Jimmy said.
"Everyone wants my candy so badly,
they are willing to do whatever
I want to get it!"

The next day Jimmy brought
a new batch of candy to school.
Everyone was very happy to see him.
Miss Fowl let Jimmy decide
what the students should study
in her class.

Coach Gruber told Jimmy he did not have to do exercises in gym class.

But when his friends began fighting
over the last pieces of candy,
Jimmy started to worry.

When Jimmy got home, he found his
parents fighting about the candy.
Tired of all the fighting, Jimmy
decided to dump all the candy into
the river.

Jimmy flew his rocket over the city
to tell everyone the news.
"Attention, Retroville," he shouted.
"There is no more candy,
  and I will not be making any more!
  Thank you!"

The people of Retroville were
waiting for Jimmy when he landed,
and they were not happy.
They wanted more candy!

They chased Jimmy all the way
to the roof of his house!
"Chopper mode, Goddard!"
Jimmy ordered. "Take me to the
most deserted place in town!"

23

23

Jimmy and Goddard landed at
the Candy Bar, but the mob was
right behind them.
"What am I going to do?"
Jimmy wondered.
"Think . . . think. . . ."

Visions of his friends gobbling down
his candy danced in Jimmy's mind.
"Brain Blast!" he suddenly shouted.

"I've got it!" he told the candy store owner. "Lab mice can be trained not to eat something if it causes them pain. Keep everybody here—our problems are solved!"

A little later Jimmy stood
on the roof of the Candy Bar.
"Ladies and gentlemen," he called
down to the crowd,
"I give you all the candy you want!"

The people of Retroville were
overjoyed with the candy . . . until
they realized that every bite
delivered an electric shock!
"Ow, ow!" they yelled.
"It's delicious, but it's too painful
to eat!"

Three days later everyone was still
throwing out the last of the candy.
"Putting my edible batteries in
   every piece of candy was a great
   idea," Jimmy told Carl.
"It did not take long for people to
   see that eating my candy just was
   not worth the pain!"
"I am just glad everyone is back
   to normal," Carl said.

"Hey, Jimmy—buzz!" Sheen said,
walking over to them, eating
a piece of Jimmy's candy.
"That last batch of candy—buzz!—
was delicious!
Got any—buzz!—more?"
Jimmy looked at Carl and shrugged.
"Well, almost everyone is back
to normal. . . ."